D1326564

TYRONE
THE DIRTY ROTTEN CHEAT

BY HANS WILHELM

Scholastic Hardcover
Scholastic Publications Limited
London

Scholastic Publications Ltd.,
10 Earlham Street, London WC2H 9RX, UK

Scholastic Inc.,
730 Broadway, New York, NY 10003, USA

Scholastic Canada Ltd.,
123 Newkirk Road, Richmond Hill,
Ontario L4C 3G5, Canada

Ashton Scholastic Pty. Ltd.,
P O Box 579, Gosford, New South Wales,
Australia

Ashton Scholastic Ltd.,
Private Bag 1, Penrose, Auckland,
New Zealand

Published in the US by Scholastic Inc, USA 1991.
Published in the UK by Scholastic Publications Ltd, 1991.

ISBN 0 590 76535 3

Made and printed by Proost International Bookproduction

To Eva Moore

Boland was a little dinosaur.
He and his friends were going to Swamp Island for a week.
They would eat, play games, and sleep out under the stars.
Everybody was very excited. Everybody that is, except Boland.
His worst enemy, Tyrone, was coming along too!
Tyrone the Horrible, as he was usually called,
was known to make trouble. Lots of trouble.

Tyrone was just a kid himself,
but he was bigger and stronger than the others.

No wonder he won the first game so easily.

They played other games that had nothing to do
with being big or strong.
Still, Tyrone won every time.
"Something is not quite right here,"
Boland thought.

Tyrone didn't seem to care what anyone thought.
He played by his very own rules.
For instance, in the game of meteorite bowling,
he just stepped over the white line when no one was
looking. He was soon the meteorite bowling champion.

"Ha ha!" Tyrone said to himself. "Cheating is easy – as long as nobody finds out."

Meanwhile, Boland and his friends were upset.
They had lost all their meteorites to Tyrone.
"How did he do it?" Stego said, shaking his head.

"I'm sure that he cheated!" replied Terry.

"I think so, too," said Boland.
"Next time we will watch him more closely.
We have to catch him red-handed."

The next game was the great dinosaur egg race.
It was Boland's favourite.
Towards the end Boland was in the lead,
closely followed by Tyrone. Suddenly Boland stumbled
and fell over something big and green.
It was Tyrone's foot!

"You spiteful animal!" cried Boland.
But Tyrone was already crossing the finishing line with a big smile on his face.

“He is not the winner!” Boland told his friends.
“Didn’t you see how he tripped me?”
But nobody had seen it. They had all been
too busy watching their eggs.

Naturally Tyrone swore he hadn’t done anything wrong.
And so they had to give him the first prize,
which was a delicious chocolate egg.

Once again Tyrone was pleased with himself.
"Yes, indeed, cheating always works.
All you have to do is tell a big fat lie!"

“Time for the sack race!” Stella called.

“Count me out,” said Boland.
“I’m not playing any more games with Tyrone.”

Nobody else wanted to play with Tyrone either.
But Stella said, “Don’t be silly. Nobody can cheat in a sack race. Besides, the winner gets the best prize of all – a big chocolate dinosaur.”

Everyone wanted to win the chocolate dinosaur, and soon the race was on.
But, believe it or not – once again, Tyrone came in first!

Tyrone went off by himself to enjoy his prize.
But this time Boland followed him
and discovered his secret.
Tyrone's sack was cut open at the bottom!
He had not hopped like the others –
he ran the race!

"You dirty rotten cheat!" Boland cried.
"Give back that chocolate dinosaur.
You don't deserve it."

Then Tyrone got mean.
"You'd better shut up, Lizardhead," he said.
"If you say one word about this to anyone else,
you'll be sorry."

But Boland told his friends everything.
"I'm fed up with that brute," he said,
and stamped his foot.
"But what can we do?" Stella asked.
"Tyrone is so big and strong."

"If Tyrone can't play fair," Boland said,
"we'll cut him out of the next game.
I have an idea. Let's meet tonight
after Tyrone goes to sleep."

GC
HE

That night around the camp fire Boland told the others his idea. "Listen, everybody. This is a map of Swamp Island, and here is the spot where I have buried a special surprise."

"Hooray! A treasure hunt. What a great idea!" Stego cried. "What kind of a surprise is it?"

"I can't tell you. It's a secret," said Boland. "You will have to wait until tomorrow. The treasure hunt will begin first thing in the morning.

"But," he said, "don't say anything to that cheat Tyrone. I don't want him to spoil the surprise."

Boland didn't know it,
but Tyrone had heard everything.
And he was not about to wait
until morning.

Later that night,
when the other dinosaurs were sleeping,
he took the map and a shovel...

...and sneaked off into the dark.

The sun was about to come up
by the time Tyrone found the spot.
"Aha!" he said. "I win again.
Now the treasure will be mine. All MINE!"

Tyrone started to dig wildly.
He didn't look where he was
throwing the dirt.
He didn't see the swarm
of bees behind him
until it was too late.

“AAARRRUUUGGG!” Tyrone yelled as the angry bees went after him. “Help! Help!”

The other dinosaurs heard his cries and came running.

When they saw the map and the shovel,
they knew what had happened.

"Tyrone tried to beat us again," Terry said.
"He wanted the surprise for himself."

"It looks like he got a surprise all right,"
Boland said with a smile.

That evening there was a big party on Swamp Island.
The treasure box had been full of fireworks –
and Boland and his friends enjoyed the spectacular show.
But Tyrone was not happy. He was so sore from his bee stings
he had to stay in the water all night.